39 Kids on the Block

Chicken Pox Strikes Again

Look for these and other books in the
39 Kids on the Block series:

39 Kids on the Block™

Chicken Pox Strikes Again

by Jean Marzollo

illustrated by Irene Trivas

SCHOLASTIC INC.
New York   Toronto   London   Auckland   Sydney

ISBN 0-590-42727-X

12 11 10 9 8 7 6 5 4 3 2 1   0 1 2 3 4 5/9

Printed in CANADA   11

First Scholastic Printing, June 1990

For Grace Maccarone
and
Jean Feiwel

With special thanks to
Janet Barton, Rosemary Wells,
Harriet Egertson, Becky Beane,
and her father-in-law, the real
Sydney Beane, a Yankton Sioux,
who collected Indian legends
and was never sharp to
his grandchildren.
— J.M.

For Fanny, Peter, and Becca
— I.T.

Thirty-nine kids live on Baldwin Street.
They range in age from babies to teenagers.
The main kids in this story are:
John Beane,
Fizz Eddie Fox,
Susan Beane,
Bob Beane,
Rusty Morelli,
Lisa Wu,
Maria Lopez,
Jane Fox,
Mary Kate Adams,
Michael Finn

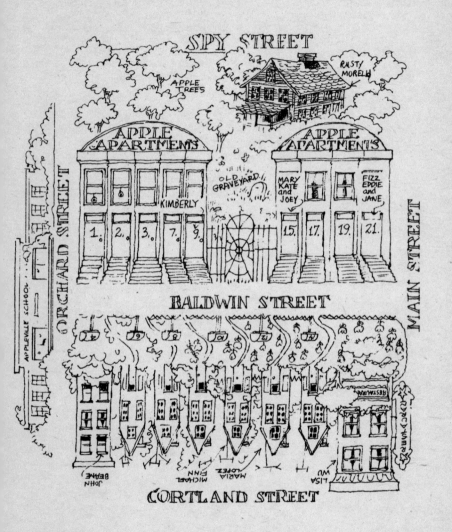

Chapter 1

Fizz Eddie sat down next to John Beane. "How's the story going?" he asked.

Fizz Eddie was in junior high. He was John's reading partner. He was called Fizz Eddie because he was good at phys ed.

Once a week Fizz Eddie and other teenagers came to John's class. They helped the kids read and write.

Sometimes they read books to their partners. They read chapter books and picture books.

Fizz Eddie and John liked picture books best. Their favorite author was Rosemary Wells because she was funny. Their favorite book by her was about a rabbit named Max and a chocolate chicken.

John Beane took some papers out from his desk. "It's all done," he said.

"Great," said Fizz Eddie. "Let's hear it. I'll pretend I'm Rosemary Wells."

John Beane began to read softly. He wanted only Fizz Eddie to hear.

Other kids were reading quietly to their partners, too.

At the Author's Tea stories would be read aloud to everyone. But for now they were secret.

John had been working on his story for two weeks. He wanted it to be really funny.

After all, Rosemary Wells was coming to the tea! She was going to be the visiting author.

John still couldn't believe it.

He and Fizz Eddie had suggested her. And Mr. Carson had said, "Why don't you write and invite her?"

So they did. Way back in October they wrote her a funny letter. And she wrote a funny letter back saying she could come.

Now the Authors' Tea was only two weeks away. Everyone in the class was very excited.

But writing was hard work.

John's printing was wobbly.

And for a long time he didn't have a good enough idea. Everything he wrote seemed boring.

Then Fizz Eddie told him a joke. And John had his story.

He had shown the rough draft to Fizz Eddie. Fizz Eddie had laughed.

John showed it to Mr. Carson, and Mr. Carson laughed, too. He said John should list Fizz Eddie as the co-author.

Mr. Carson also made a few corrections in red ink. Then John copied the whole thing over. When he was finished, he felt very proud.

Now he read it aloud—softly.

Shut Up and Trouble
by John Beane and Fizz Eddie Fox

Once there was a man named Trouble. He had a friend named Shut Up. One day Trouble got lost. Shut Up drove around and around looking for him. He was driving very fast.

A police officer stopped him and said, "What's your name?"

Shut Up said to the police officer, "Shut up."

That made the police officer mad. He said, "Are you looking for trouble?"

Shut up said, "Yes I am. Can you tell me where he is?"

"Who are you?" said the officer.

"I told you before," said Shut Up. "SHUT UP!"

Fizz Eddie put his arm around John. "My name is Rosemary Wells," he said. "And I think your story is perfect."

John felt wonderful.

"All you have to do is make a few pictures of those dudes and a cover," said Fizz Eddie. "Then you'll be ready to publish."

To publish his book, John would take it to the library. There Miss O'Brien would feed his cover pages into a little machine. They would come out covered with shiny plastic.

Then she would hold his pages and covers together and stick them into another machine. This machine would fasten the pages with a red plastic binding.

John's story would be a real book.

At the Author's Tea he and the other kids would read their stories aloud to Rosemary Wells.

And then she was going to read them a

new book that she had written.

"Do you really think Rosemary Wells will like it?" John asked Fizz Eddie.

"If she doesn't, we'll never read *Max's Chocolate Chicken* again," said Fizz Eddie.

Chapter 2

"John, why aren't you eating?"

Grampa Beane's voice was sharp. His gray braids hung straight down the front of his shirt.

"I'm not hungry," said John.

That was a lie. After school John had gone to the town pool with Rusty and Mrs. Morelli. They had stayed there for two hours. And now he was starving.

But something new was on his plate. His mother called it "Dinner in a Dish." She said she had cooked everything together in one pot.

John's grandfather was staring at him.

"I sort of like it," said his younger sister Susan. She put a little bite into her mouth.

John looked at her plate. She had hardly eaten anything.

"It's delicious," said his little brother Bob. His plate was almost full.

But Grampa Beane didn't say anything to them. He just kept staring at John.

John picked up his fork. Very carefully, he separated the hamburger from the beans, corn, tomatoes, and green pepper.

"What are you doing?" asked Grampa Beane.

"I don't like things touching," said John.

John now had five fairly neat piles on his plate. But not neat enough. There was corn in the green-pepper pile. Tomatoes in the meat.

"Start with the corn," said his mother. She was still dressed in her police uniform. "Wash it down with milk."

That might work.

John stabbed a kernel of corn with his

fork. He wiped it off with his napkin. Then he put it between his teeth and bit half off. He took a big gulp of milk.

"Go to your room," said his grandfather. "You eat like an ant. Come back when you can eat like a horse."

John's eyes filled with tears. He blinked. A drop fell on his cheek. John wiped it away quickly. He hoped no one had seen.

"Are you crying?" asked Susan.

John glowered at her. Why couldn't she keep her big mouth shut?

"I said go," said his grandfather.

John looked at his mother. She raised her eyebrows and shrugged.

He looked at his father. His father was dressed in his running clothes. He had a sit-down office job so he jogged after work. Jogging made him hungry. He was helping himself to seconds.

John left the room. He was so mad, he felt like running down the hall and slamming the door.

But if he did, his grandfather wouldn't have let him come back to the table for a week. Grampa Beane didn't like temper tantrums.

That was only one of the many things his grandfather didn't like.

John peeked in his grandfather's room. It had a small bed and a desk.

His grandfather was an author. But not a funny author like Rosemary Wells.

His grandfather wrote serious books for grownups. They were all about American Indians.

All the pictures in his room were of Indians. There were no pictures of cowboys or army soldiers. Grampa Beane didn't like cowboys and soldiers. He said they had stolen land from the Indians.

There was one picture John loved.

It was of an Indian long ago sitting on a horse. He was looking over a vast herd of buffalos. His headdress touched his feet.

If Grampa had lived in the olden days,

he might have been happier, thought John.

John's bedroom was between his grandfather's room and his parents' room.

Some kids only lived with one grownup. Some lived with two. But John lived with three.

He was surrounded.

And not just with grown-ups.

He had to share his room with his brother and sister.

His friends Michael Finn and Rusty Morelli were lucky. They each had their own rooms.

And they didn't have brothers, sisters, and crabby grandfathers to bother them.

Someone knocked on John's door.

"Come in," said John.

It was his mom. She sat on the side of the bed. "I didn't like that 'Dinner in a Dish' much either," she said. "But I ate it anyway. There's no point in making a fuss. Especially when you're hungry. And you are hungry, right?"

John nodded. He was glad his mother had come to see him.

"Why didn't Grampa say something to Susan and Bob?" he asked. "They weren't eating either."

"You're older," said his mother. "He expects you to set a good example for them."

John hated that reason.

But there was no point in saying anything. They had been over this topic before.

So he said, "Do I have to eat everything?"

"Half," said his mom.

So John went back to the table. By then, everyone else was gone.

Susan and Bob were playing in the living room. John's grandfather was watching the weather on TV. And his dad was washing dishes.

John wished Grampa Beane was still at the table. Because once he got going, he did okay. He washed each bite down with milk. And before he knew it, he had eaten everything.

He wanted to make his grandfather proud of him. But he couldn't tell his grandfather what he'd done. Grampa Beane would think he was bragging.

Bragging was another thing Grampa Beane didn't like.

When it came right down to it, there wasn't one thing John could think of that his grandfather liked.

He didn't know how to make him happy.

Rusty's grandmother, Mrs. Morelli, was completely different. She was like a kid. That afternoon she had jumped off the high dive.

And do you know what she had said afterwards?

She said, "I bet I'm the only grandmother in New Jersey who can do that."

She had bragged.

Rusty was really lucky.

Chapter 3

"Everybody stand up and stretch," said Mr. Carson.

John and the rest of the kids stood up. They reached their hands into the air and tried to touch the ceiling.

Mr. Carson said, "You can stretch much higher in June than you could in September."

Then, because Mr. Carson was Mr. Carson, he had to get out a measuring tape and measure everyone. Mr. Carson loved math. Any chance to use numbers made him happy.

Mr. Carson put up a chart that showed everyone's height in September.

The kids compared their old measurements with their new ones.

"I grew two inches," said Rusty.

"I grew an inch and a half," said Lisa.

"I didn't grow at all," said Maria.

Neither did I, thought John.

"Don't feel bad, Maria," said Mr. Carson. "Height is not the only way to grow. How else can a person grow? Let's brainstorm a list."

He wrote on the board: *Growing Chart.* Underneath he wrote: *How many ways can you grow?*

Mr. Carson loved making lists, too. As long as the lists were numbered.

"Number one. You can grow fatter," said Jane Fox.

Great, thought John. He didn't want to grow that way. He wanted to grow tall.

"Number two. You can grow long hair," said Maria.

John didn't want long hair either. He wanted to be modern like his parents. Not old-fashioned like his grandfather.

"Number three. You can grow better at swimming," said Rusty.

John already knew how to swim.

"Number four. You can grow better at writing stories," said Maria.

"Absolutely," said Mr. Carson. He wrote Maria's words on the board.

Then he frowned.

"Oh dear," he said. "That reminds me. I have some bad news."

Mr. Carson picked up a pink envelope from his desk. He took out a pink letter and read it aloud.

Dear Mr. Carson and Children,

Last week I fell and broke my leg. I hate to cancel at this late date. But I won't be able to come to your Author's Tea next week.

Thank you for inviting me. May I make a suggestion? Invite Sidney Beane. He lives in your town. He writes wonderful stories about American Indians.

Sincerely,
Rosemary Wells

John couldn't believe his ears for two reasons.

First, he couldn't believe that Rosemary Wells couldn't come. He had wanted to see if his story would make her laugh.

He had wanted to tell her some other ideas for silly stories. And he wanted to tell her a secret.

Even though his printing was wobbly,

he was thinking of being an author when he grew up.

He had never told that to anyone. Not even Fizz Eddie or his parents.

Now John wouldn't get to tell Rosemary Wells anything.

There was another reason John couldn't believe his ears. Rosemary Wells had suggested his grandfather!

"Hm-m-m," said Mr. Carson. "I wonder how we could get hold of Sidney Beane?"

John looked around. He didn't say a word. Maybe no one knew that Sidney Beane was his grandfather.

The last thing John wanted was for his grandfather to come to the Author's Tea.

Grampa Beane's stories were all sad. They were all about mean things white people had done to Indians.

They weren't stories for kids. Grampa Beane didn't even like kids.

He took care of his grandchildren after

school. But he didn't have fun doing it. He just made sure they were safe.

True, at Christmas he had come to school and blessed the Giving Tree. But that was different. He hadn't come as an author. And he hadn't stayed long.

John heard kids giggling. He turned to see what was funny.

They were all staring at him.

"Does anyone know Sidney Beane?" Mr. Carson asked again.

Suddenly John saw the twinkle in Mr. Carson's eyes.

Of course Mr. Carson knew who Sidney Beane was. He was just waiting for John to say something. The rest of the kids were waiting, too. That's why they were giggling.

"I do," John finally said.

Then he added, "But I don't think my grandfather would like to be our author."

"Why not?" asked Michael Finn. "He can read Indian legends to us."

Only Michael Finn would say "legends" instead of stories. He knew as many big words as Mr. Carson.

John shook his head. "I don't know," he mumbled.

"We could write him a letter and ask," said Mary Kate.

Everyone agreed so John kept quiet.

Lisa Wu wrote the letter because she had the best penmanship. Michael Finn decorated the letter with Indian pictographs. That was another word he knew.

Rusty rolled it up and tied it with a ribbon.

And John had to bring the dumb thing home.

Chapter 4

Grampa Beane was working in his bedroom. When he heard John and Susan come home, he came into the kitchen.

Bob was still at day care.

John fixed himself and Susan a peanut-butter sandwich.

His grandfather watched. He sat in an old rocking chair in the kitchen.

The rolled-up letter was on the counter.

John didn't say a word about it.

Susan ate half her sandwich and drank half her milk. Then she left.

Grampa Beane put the half glass of milk in the refrigerator.

Did he say anything to Susan about it? Not one word.

John finished his whole sandwich and left only an inch of milk.

"Finish your milk," said Grampa Beane.

John gritted his teeth.

He could just see it. Mr. Carson had said there would be cookies and juice at the Author's Tea. If John didn't finish his juice, his grandfather would say something about it. He would embarrass him in front of everyone.

Maybe he didn't have to give his grandfather the letter at all. He could just tell Mr. Carson the next day that his grandfather couldn't come.

"What's that?" asked Grampa Beane. He pointed at the letter.

John wanted to say, "Nothing." But he didn't dare. What if Mr. Carson called up his grandfather and asked about the tea?

John handed the letter to his grandfather. "It's for you," he said.

Grampa Beane sat down and untied the ribbon. He folded the ribbon up and put it in his pocket.

Grampa Beane never wasted anything.

Slowly he unrolled the letter and read it. When he was done, he rolled it up again. He took the ribbon out of his pocket and tied it up.

Grampa Beane started rocking back and forth. As he rocked, he tapped the rolled up letter on his leg.

"You going to come?" asked John.

"You want me to?" asked his grandfather.

Of all the things his grandfather disliked, lying was the worst.

But John always had to lie to him.

He said he wasn't hungry when he was. He told him he didn't like to play with toy soldiers. But he always played with them at Rusty's house.

And now he had to lie again.

"Yes," he said. "I want you to come. Should I tell Mr. Carson yes?"

The next day in school John read his grandfather's letter aloud.

Dear Children,

Thank you for inviting me to your Author's Tea. I would be honored to come.

Sincerely,
Sidney Beane

Everyone except John was very excited. Lisa Wu raised her hand. "Can I start a new story? It's going to be about my sister Julie and the chicken pox. You should see her. She has blisters between her toes."

"If you start a new story, you'll have to work quickly to have it ready in time," said Mr. Carson.

Then he looked worried. "I hope *you* don't catch chicken pox," he told Lisa.

John decided to start a new story, too. His grandfather wouldn't like his story about Shut Up and Trouble.

"What is your new story going to be about?" asked Mr. Carson. John decided he would write about the weather. His grandfather liked weather.

Weather
by John Beane

Sometimes it is sunny out. Sometimes it rains. Sometimes it snows. Sometimes it hails. Sometimes it's boring and gray like today.

John worked on his new story for a long time. It didn't work very well.

His grandfather liked to watch the weather.

But he probably wouldn't like John's story.

Neither did John.

Chapter 5

Sunday afternoon was hot and sunny. "Let's all go to the pool," said John's dad.

"Not me," said Grampa Beane. "Swimming pools are too modern. I like to swim in lakes high up in the mountains."

"Not too many of those around here," said John's dad. He, John's mom, Susan, Bob, and John piled into the car and left.

The pool was crowded. But John liked it that way. All his friends were there. Rusty, Michael, Maria, Mary Kate, Lisa, and Jane.

Fizz Eddie was working at the snack bar.

"Five cones," said John. "Two chocolate, two strawberry, and one double-dip fudge twirl."

"Coming up," said Fizz Eddie. "Is your grandfather here?" he asked. "Can I meet him? He sounds like an interesting guy."

"He's home writing," said John with relief. When Fizz Eddie met his grandfather, he was going to be disappointed.

"You still going to read that awful weather story at the Author's Tea?" asked Fizz Eddie.

"Shut up," said John.

The people standing next to John looked down at him. They couldn't believe he had spoken so rudely.

"What's the matter?" asked Fizz Eddie. "You looking for trouble?"

"Yes," said John. "You know where he went?"

Fizz Eddie laughed. He handed John a little cardboard tray that held the five cones. "I think he went in the pool," he said.

* * *

Monday morning the class started decorating the room for the Author's Tea on Friday.

John and Lisa made red and white paper chains. Those were the colors of the Appleville School.

As she worked, Lisa kept scratching her stomach. She said she felt hot as fire.

John touched her forehead. It was burning.

Mr. Carson asked him to take Lisa to the nurse.

Mrs. Foster put a thermometer in Lisa's mouth. Then she said, "Show me where you itch."

Lisa lifted up her jersey. Her stomach had little red bumps on it.

Mrs. Foster called Lisa's mom on the phone. "I think Lisa has the chicken pox," she said.

John was shocked. He had never seen a kid with the chicken pox.

NURSE

Lisa burst into tears. "My sister had to stay home for a week. What if I miss the Author's Tea?"

"Let's see what happens," said Mrs. Foster. "Maybe you'll have a mild case. Here's what will happen. First you get bumps. The bumps become blisters. The blisters may ooze, but soon afterwards they will crust over. Just don't scratch them! When all the blisters have crusted over, you can come back to school."

The nurse was very nice. But Lisa was still crying when John left.

Lisa had to wait in the office for her mother to pick her up.

"Lisa has the chicken pox," John told Mr. Carson. "She may not be able to come to the Author's Tea."

Mr. Carson said he was sorry to hear that.

As he said that, John began to get a crazy idea. If *he* got the chicken pox, too, he wouldn't have to go to the Author's Tea either!

"What are you smiling at?" asked Mr. Carson.

"Nothing," said John. He went back to his seat and made a boring cover for his boring weather story.

Then he took his cover down to the library. Miss O'Brien put it in the laminating machine. It came out shiny.

She put it in the binding machine. It came out a book.

It was a boring book. But so what? It would not be read aloud at the Author's Tea. Because the author would not be there.

John began to scratch his arm. "I feel hot," he said.

Miss O'Brien looked at him. "Maybe you better go to the nurse," she said.

Mary Kate went with him. "I already had the chicken pox," she said. "It was nothing."

The nurse took John's temperature. "It's normal," she said. "Let's see where you itch."

John pointed to a little dot on his arm. "Right there," he said.

"That's a beauty mark," said the nurse. "I think you're fine. Isn't that good news?"

Chapter 6

On Tuesday Rusty came down with the chicken pox. On Wednesday Jane got them.

But not John. Each time he found a dot on his skin, he went to see Mrs. Foster. Each time she said it was a beauty mark.

On Thursday the custodian brought a big table into Mr. Carson's classroom. Mr. Carson put a tablecloth on it.

Maria made paper flowers from tissue paper. She put them in decorated juice cans on the table.

John folded red napkins. He set them on the table in a neat row.

Michael put paper cups and paper plates on the table.

Mary Kate made a computer sign. It said WELCOME SIDNEY BEANE TO THE APPLEVILLE SCHOOL.

Mr. Carson hung the sign above the table. It looked great.

Even John felt a little excited. But he still didn't want to go. He looked all over his skin for spots.

There! Right inside his elbow! Yes! He raised his hand and asked to go to the nurse.

"Again?" said Mr. Carson. "All right. Who wants to go with him?"

Mary Kate went with him again. "What's the matter with you?" she asked. "Do you *want* to get chicken pox or something?"

John looked at her. He felt like telling her the truth. So he said, "Yes."

"Why?" asked Mary Kate.

"Because I want to miss the Author's Tea," said John.

"Are you serious?" asked Mary Kate. She was looking at him as if he were nuts.

Because my crabby grandfather is coming, John wanted to say. But he just couldn't.

"I don't like my story," he said.

"Write another one," said Mary Kate.

Suddenly John felt very tired. He was tired of getting ready for the Author's Tea. He was tired of going to the nurse's office. He was tired of everything.

Mrs. Foster stuck the thermometer under his tongue. "Let's see your stomach," she said.

John shut his eyes and lifted his shirt. He was even tired of looking for spots.

"I think you've got it this time," said the nurse.

John was shocked. He looked at his tummy. Sure enough, it was covered with little red dots. And Mrs. Foster was calling Grampa Beane.

He couldn't believe he was really sick.

Grampa Beane came to pick him up. They walked home together.

"I guess you'll miss the Author's Tea," said his grandfather.

John looked up at him.

Grampa Beane seemed sad.

"I guess so," said John.

He was surprised to find that he felt a little sad, too.

But not that sad.

Chapter 7

Friday was the day of the Author's Tea.

That morning Grampa Beane brought a tray to John's room. On the tray was tea, milk, sugar, and two tea cups.

"Your father, Susan, and Bob have left," said Grampa Beane. "Your mother will stay home with you while I go to the Author's Tea. How do you feel?"

"A little itchy," said John. "But I'm trying not to scratch."

Grampa Beane fixed him a cup of tea with a little sugar and lots of milk.

He was wearing his best ribbon shirt. John's mom had made it for him. She had made one for John and his dad, too. He also had on a bolo tie with a silver tie clasp and a hat with a beaded band.

He looks great, thought John.

Back when he thought Rosemary Wells was coming, John had planned to dress up for the tea, too.

He was going to wear his ribbon shirt and his new cowboy boots.

"I don't have to go to your school for another hour," said Grampa Beane. "Before I leave, you and I can have our own Author's Tea. I'll read you my story, and you can read me your story."

"My story is at school," said John.

"Do you know it by heart?" asked his grandfather. "Many Indians can tell their stories from memory."

John thought about it. "Actually I do," he said.

"Let's hear it," said Grampa Beane.

The thought of saying his stupid weather story out loud made John feel rotten.

"I'm too itchy," he said.

"Then we'll have our Author's Tea in the bathroom," said Grampa Beane. "While you have a baking-soda bath."

Grampa Beane filled the tub with warm water and poured a cup of baking soda.

John sat in the tub. He felt much better.

His grandfather sat on the toilet seat.

John had to laugh. This was a pretty funny Author's Tea. Rosemary Wells would have loved it.

"Okay, here's my story," said John. He knew he had to get it over with.

"Weather," he said. "Sometimes it is sunny out. Sometimes it rains. Sometimes it snows. Sometimes it hails. Sometimes it's boring and gray like today."

Grampa Beane didn't say a word.

John stared at the water in the tub. He was embarrassed that his story was so bad.

But at least it was over with.

And soon Grampa Beane would go to school. And come home. And then the Author's Tea would be over with, too.

John didn't care. He didn't want to be an author any more anyway.

"One bright summer day all the flowers were out," said his grandfather.

John looked up at him. His grandfather was looking out the bathroom window. He had a faraway look on his face.

"The flowers were nodding their heads in the breeze. They were showing each other their many beautiful colors.

"But one flower was sad. 'What will happen to us when winter comes?' she asked. 'Will we all die? It doesn't seem fair. All summer long we make the world

beautiful. When we die, we should have a happy hunting ground of our own to go to.'

"The Mighty Spirit heard the unhappy flower and thought she was right. The Mighty Spirit decided that flowers should not die when winter comes.

"So now after a shower, we see a rainbow in the sky. It is the happy hunting ground of the flowers."

Grampa Beane closed his eyes. He looked peaceful and happy.

John said, "Is that the story you're going to tell at school?"

"Yes," said Grampa Beane.

"I thought you would tell a sad story," said John.

"Not to children," said Grampa Beane. "Children are the flowers of the earth."

John was surprised at this.

"You mean children like me?" he asked. "Do I seem like a flower to you?"

"You are a sunflower that is learning to stand up tall," said Grampa Beane. "Your story about weather brings honor to our family."

"It does?" asked John. Now he was really surprised.

"It is Indian poetry," said Grampa Beane. "I have memorized it. Listen."

Sometimes it is sunny out.
Sometimes it rains.
Sometimes it snows.
Sometimes it hails.
Sometimes it's boring and gray
Like today.

His grandfather made the words sound beautiful. John felt good inside.

He thought of more things to say about the weather. John said them out loud. As he said them, he tried to sound like his grandfather.

Sometimes it pours.
Sometimes it's sweaty.
Sometimes it's quiet.
And sometimes . . . it's itchy!

John ducked his head under the water. He couldn't believe he'd said that silly last line.

He didn't want to come up out of the water. He knew his grandfather would be mad at him.

But John had to get a breath of air.

He popped out of the water and heard his grandfather laughing.

John opened his eyes. His grandfather had a big grin on his face. "That was very good, John," he said. "May I tell your poem to your class?"

"Sure!" said John. His heart filled with happiness. But then, like a balloon, it popped.

Suddenly he felt as bad as Lisa, Rusty, and Jane.

Like them, he wanted to go to the Author's Tea.

But like them, he was struck down with chicken pox.

Chapter 8

Ten days later, John put on his ribbon shirt and new boots.

He was so glad to be going back to school that he decided to dress up. Author's Tea or no Author's Tea.

When he got to school, he reported to the nurse's office. He showed Mrs. Foster that all his spots were dry.

Then he saw Fizz Eddie in the hall.

"We missed you at the tea," said Fizz Eddie. "Your grandfather is cool."

John nodded.

Michael and Mary Kate had called him and said the same thing.

The word Michael had used was "impressive."

"Your grampa told us your weather poem," said Fizz Eddie. "You're a poet. And didn't know it." He laughed. "See? I'm a poet, too."

John laughed. It was great to be back at school.

His classroom seemed like another kind of home. He was glad to be back there with all his friends.

"I had so many spots, I couldn't count them all," said Jane.

"Not as many as I had," said Lisa. "I was covered."

Actually John's doctor had said that John's case was one of the worst he had ever seen. But John didn't say that. He didn't want to brag.

He was just glad that the nasty itching was over with.

"What did you do when you were home?" asked Mr. Carson. "Did you write any more poems?"

"I'm a poet. And didn't know it," said John.

Mr. Carson laughed.

"We wrote your grandfather thank-you notes," he said. "Will you take them home to him?"

Mary Kate showed John the notes. They were put together in a book.

Michael had made the cover. On it he had drawn a picture of Grampa Beane. You could see his braids, his ribbon shirt, and his tie.

John opened the book. Each student had written a letter. Each letter was decorated with pictures. Many of the pictures were of rainbows made of flowers.

John read some of the letters aloud.

Dear Mr. Beane,

Thank you for reading us the story about the rainbow. It made me happy.

Love,
Mary Kate Adams

Dear Sidney Beane,

I am deeply grateful to you for attending our outstanding Author's Tea. Would you please consider mentioning my name in one of your stories?

Your admiring fan,
Michael Finn

Dear Mr. Beane,

My name is Maria. I love your story. I love your shirt. I love you.

Love,
Maria Lopez

John was as proud as an eagle.

But one thing was odd. The last page in the book was blank.

"What is that page for?" he asked.

"We thought you might want to write something," said Mr. Carson.

John smiled. That was a good idea.

Maybe he should write about Shut Up and Trouble there.

That was possible.

Grampa Beane might like it.

But just then, another idea crept into John's mind. It was a seed of an idea that grew into a flower. And then into a rainbow.

John got out his crayons. He drew an Indian sitting on a horse. The Indian was wearing a ribbon shirt and a headdress that reached to his feet.

He and his horse were high on a mountain. They looked over a lake and a field of flowers.

Then John began to write.

Dear Grampa,

Thank you for our special Author's Tea. You know the one I mean. The one in the bathroom.

Your loving grandson,
John

Everyone wanted to know about the tea in the bathroom so John told them.

The kids were amazed.

"Can I ask a question?" said Michael.

John said sure. When he was sick, he had missed Michael. Michael always asked interesting questions.

"I already know some Indian legends," said Michael. "So if I get a ribbon shirt, can I be an Indian, too?"

"It's not what you wear," said John. "It's what you are. You can only be born an Indian." These were words he had heard his grandfather say many times.

"You're lucky to be an Indian," said Rusty.

"I know," said John.

Suddenly his eye caught the Growing Chart on the wall.

Number five, thought John. You can grow in the way you feel about yourself.

But he didn't say anything.

Because he knew he had grown a lot.

And he didn't want to brag.

About the Author

"I like writing about children and their families," says author Jean Marzollo. "Children are never boring. Whenever I get stuck for an idea, I visit a classroom and talk to the kids. They give me millions of ideas and all I have to do is choose the right one.

"I also like writing about schools and neighborhoods, which are like great big families. People who go to school together and live together learn a lot from each other. They learn to respect each other's differences. Some of my best friends today are people I grew up and went to school with.

"I remember everything about elementary school—my teacher's names, the lamp with painted roses on it that we gave the teacher when she got married, who cried and why on the playground, and how to make fish with fingerpaint.

"When I write the stories for *39 Kids on the Block*, I draw on my childhood memories and my experience in schools today. I also live with my two teenage sons and husband in Cold Spring, New York, a community with strong values and lots of stories."

Jean Marzollo has written many picture books, easy-to-read books, and novels for children. She has also written books about children for parents and teachers and articles in *Parents Magazine*.

About the Illustrator

"Jean Marzollo and I have been the best of friends for more than twenty years and we have also worked together on many books," says illustrator Irene Trivas. "She writes about kids, I draw them.

"Once upon a time we both lived in New York and learned all about living in the city. Then we moved away. I went off to Vermont and had to learn how to live in the country. But the kids we met were the same everywhere: complicated, funny, silly, serious, and more imaginative than any grown-up can ever be."

Irene Trivas has illustrated a number of picture books and easy-to-read books for children. She has also written and illustrated her own book, *Emma's Christmas: An Old Song* (Orchard).

Here are some other books about the
39 Kids on the Block:

#1 *The Green Ghost of Appleville*

Poor Rusty Morelli. He just moved into a
haunted house. Should Mary Kate help
him? Or should she just stay away?

#2 *The Best Present Ever*

Mary Kate, Jane, Rusty, and Michael all
want to get the best present ever! So
who will be the luckiest kid on the
block?

#3 *Roses Are Pink and You Stink!*

Michael Finn is angry. Everyone laughed
at him. But Michael has an idea — and
they'll be sorry!

Maria wants to cry. She wants to be Mary Kate's best friend. But Mary Kate is in a special club and Maria can't be in it!

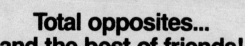